Evan Turk

heartbeat

 Atheneum Books for Young Readers • New York London Toronto Sydney New Delhi

One heart beats.

Two hearts beat.

heartbeat...

heartbeat...

Two hearts,

one song.

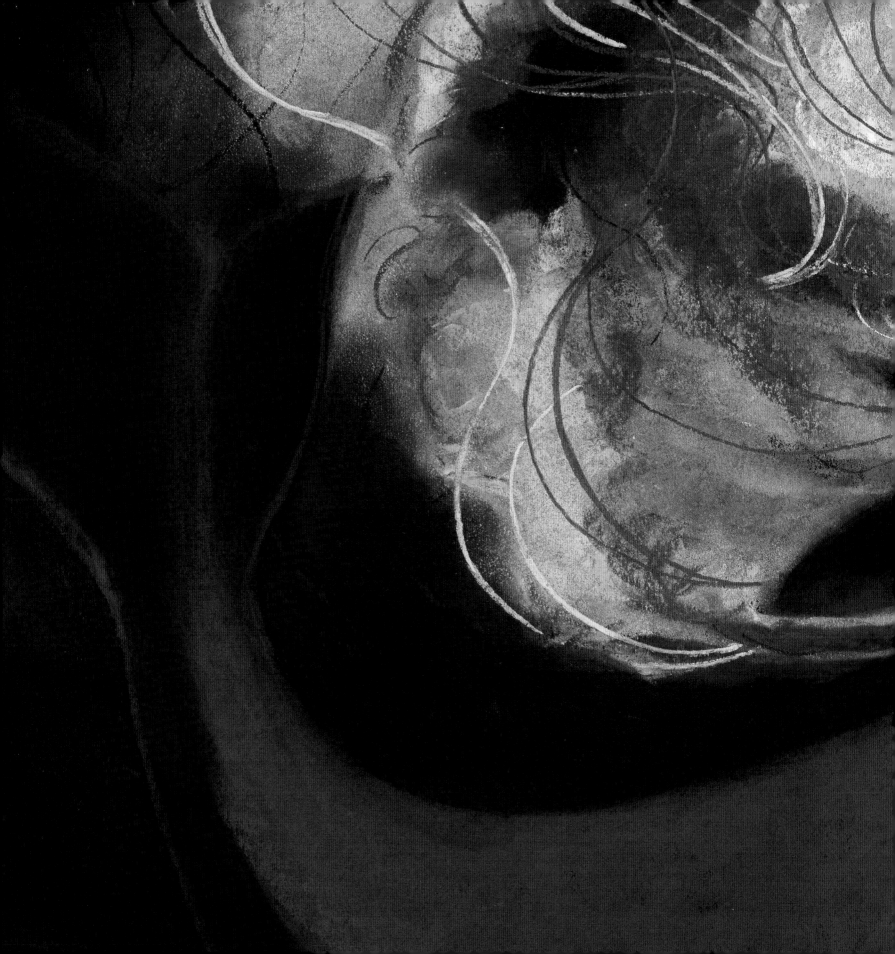

One ocean,

one song.

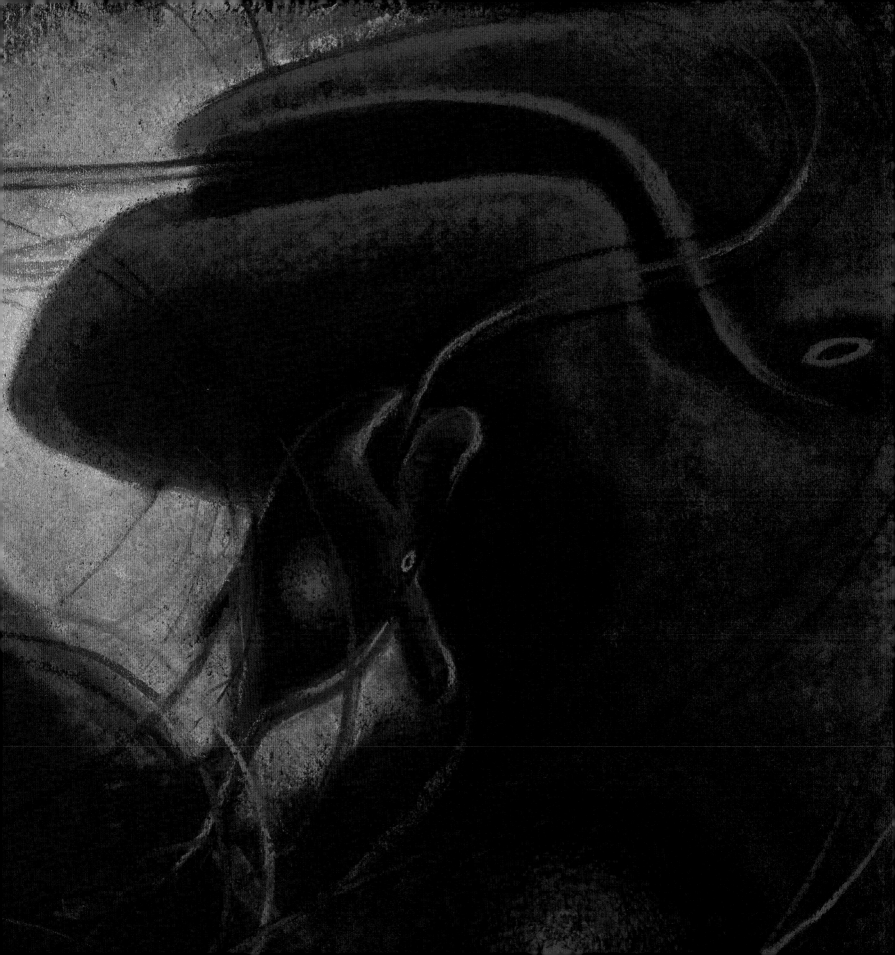

beat
beat

beat   beat   beat

beat   beat   .   beat

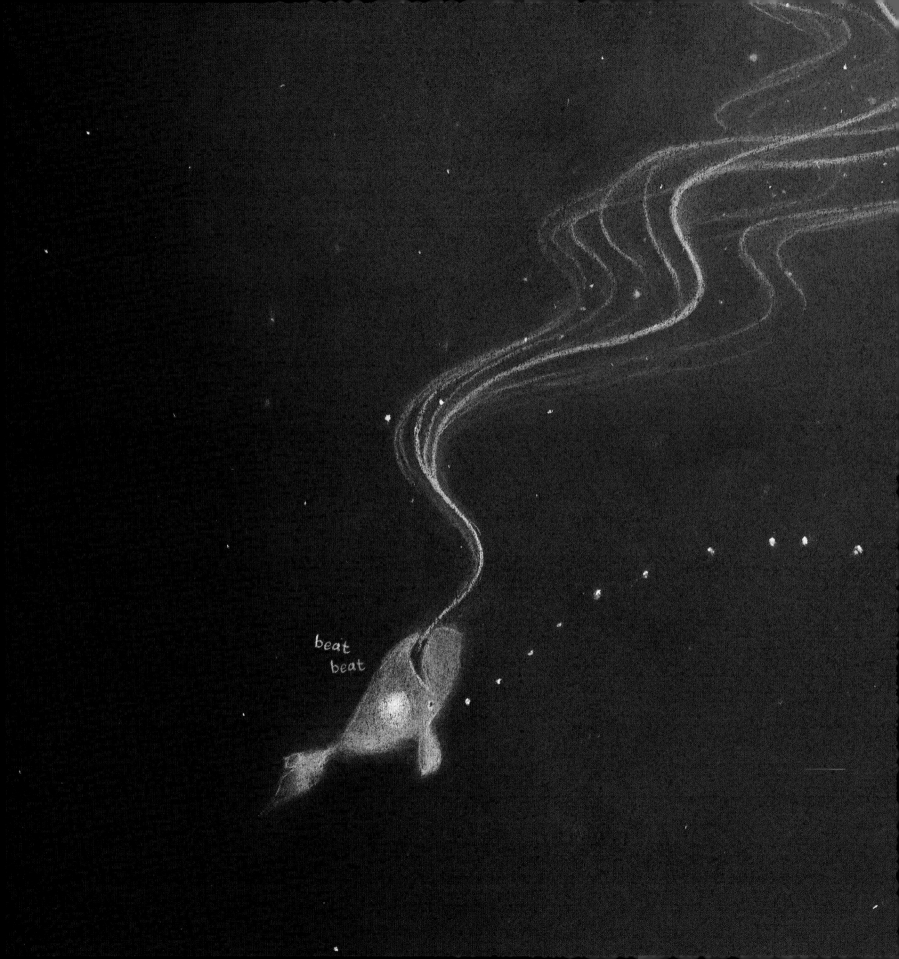

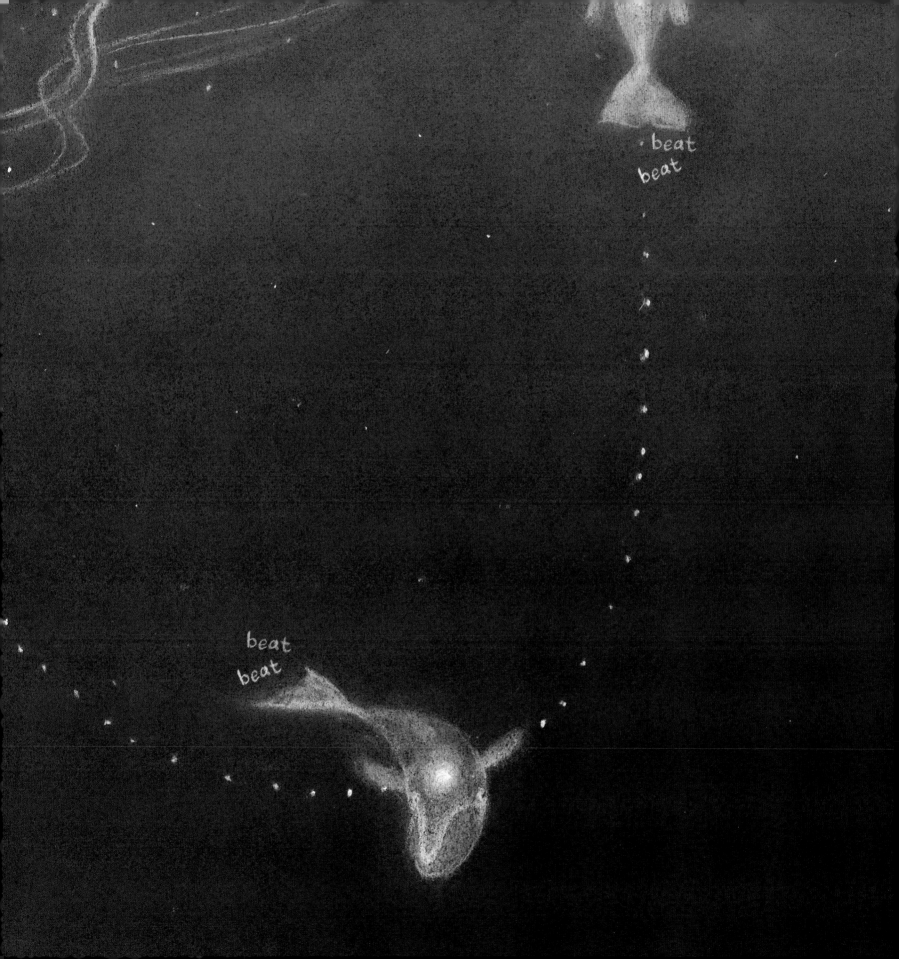

beat

heart

One heart,   one song.

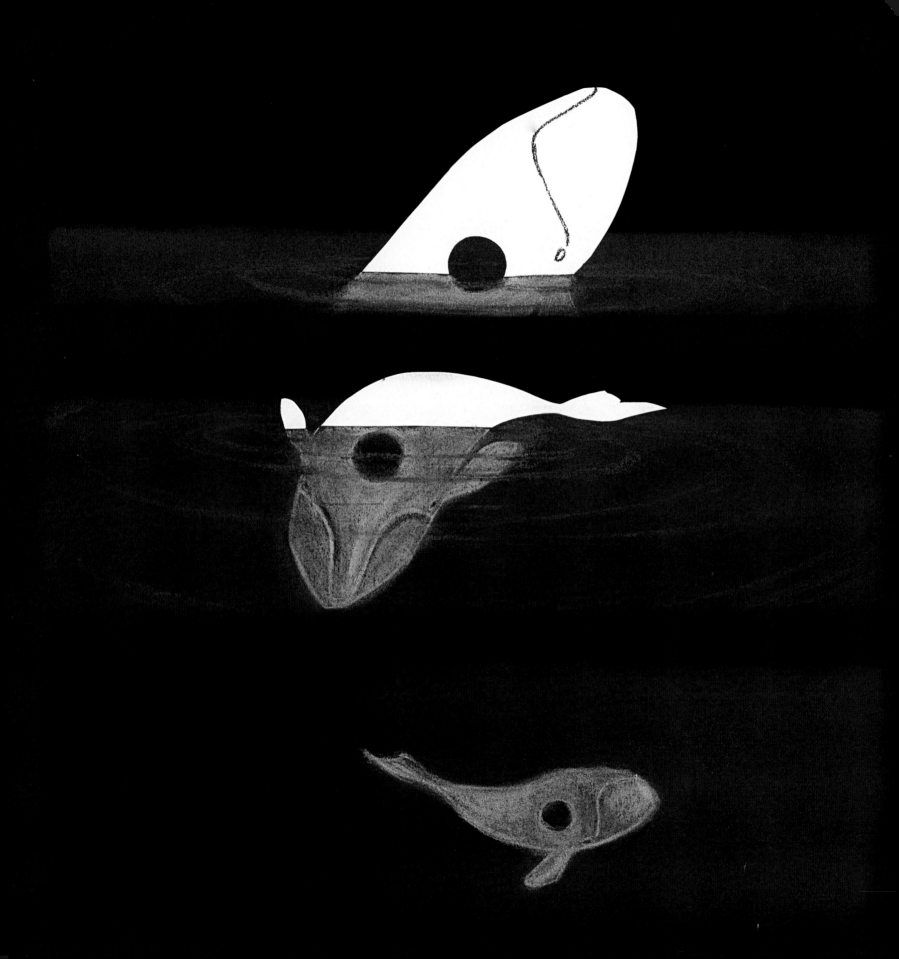

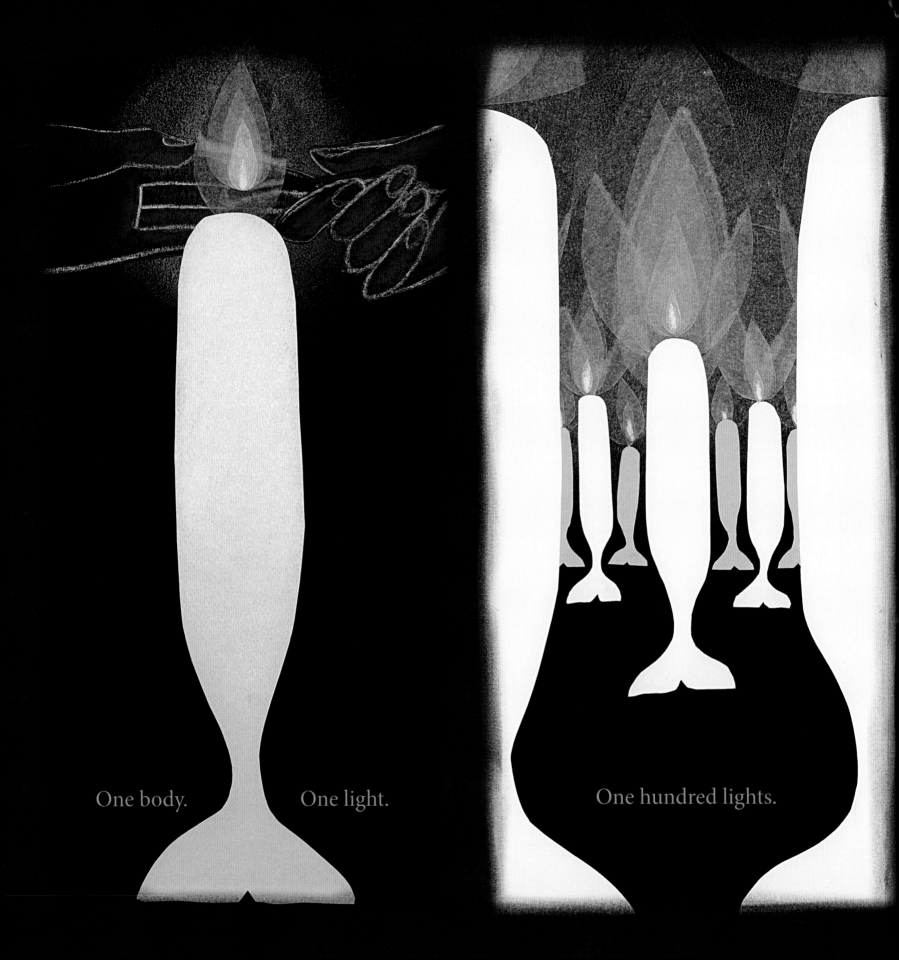

One body.   One light.

One hundred lights.

One thousand lights.   One million lights.

One million machines oiled.

Two wars fought.
One million guns shot,
bombs dropped,
mouths fed,
lives lost.
One hundred years passed.

238,900 miles traveled.

One million eyes opened.
One giant leap for mankind.

One planet, one song.
One message across the cosmic ocean.
One planet, one responsibility.

One promise to protect.

One chance to learn.

...heartbeat... ...heartbeat...

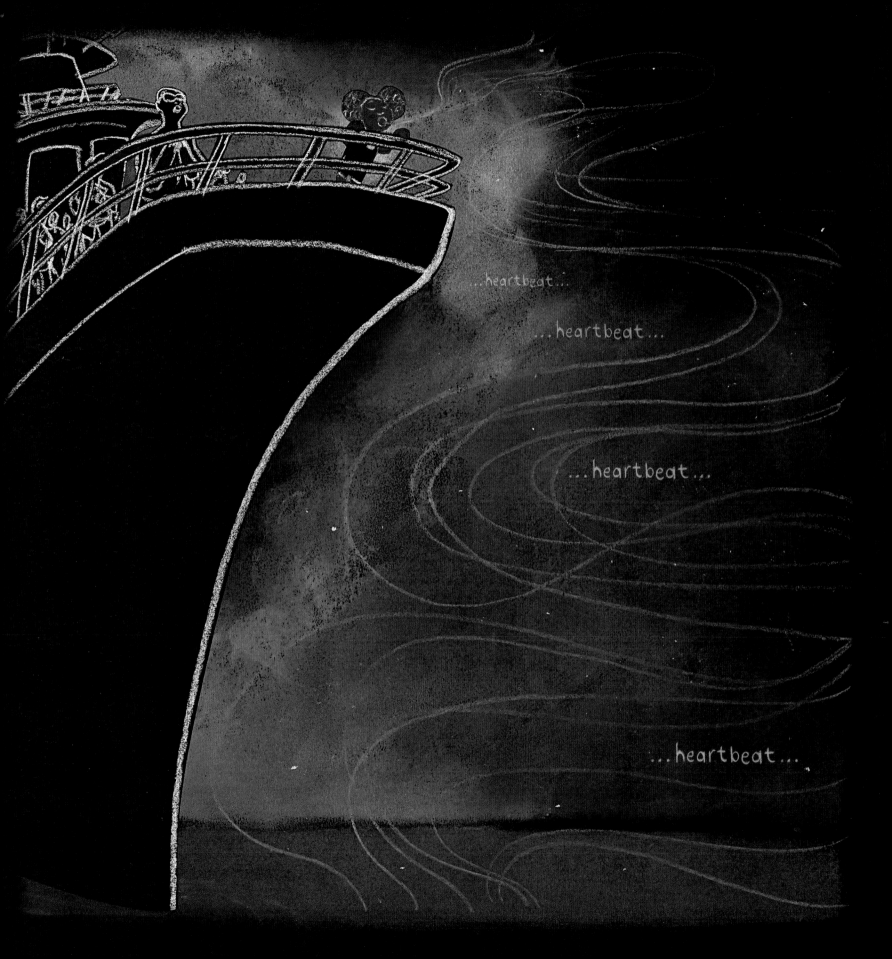

...heartbeat...

...heartbeat...

...heartbeat...

...heartbeat...

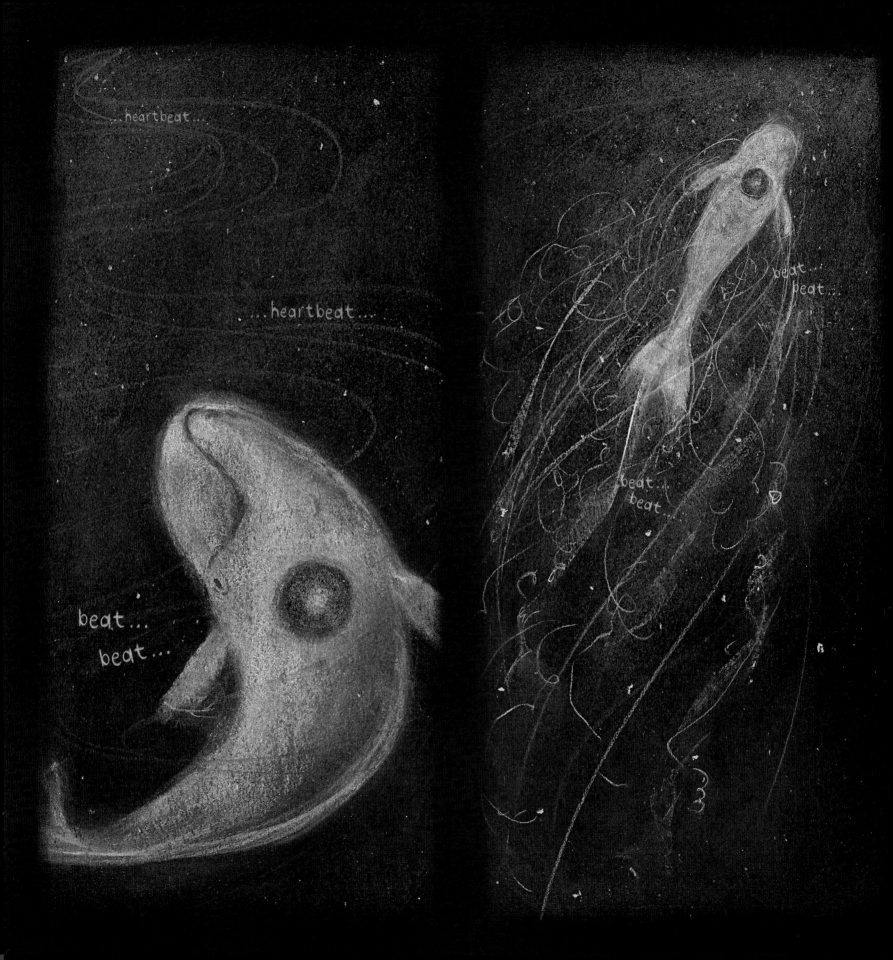

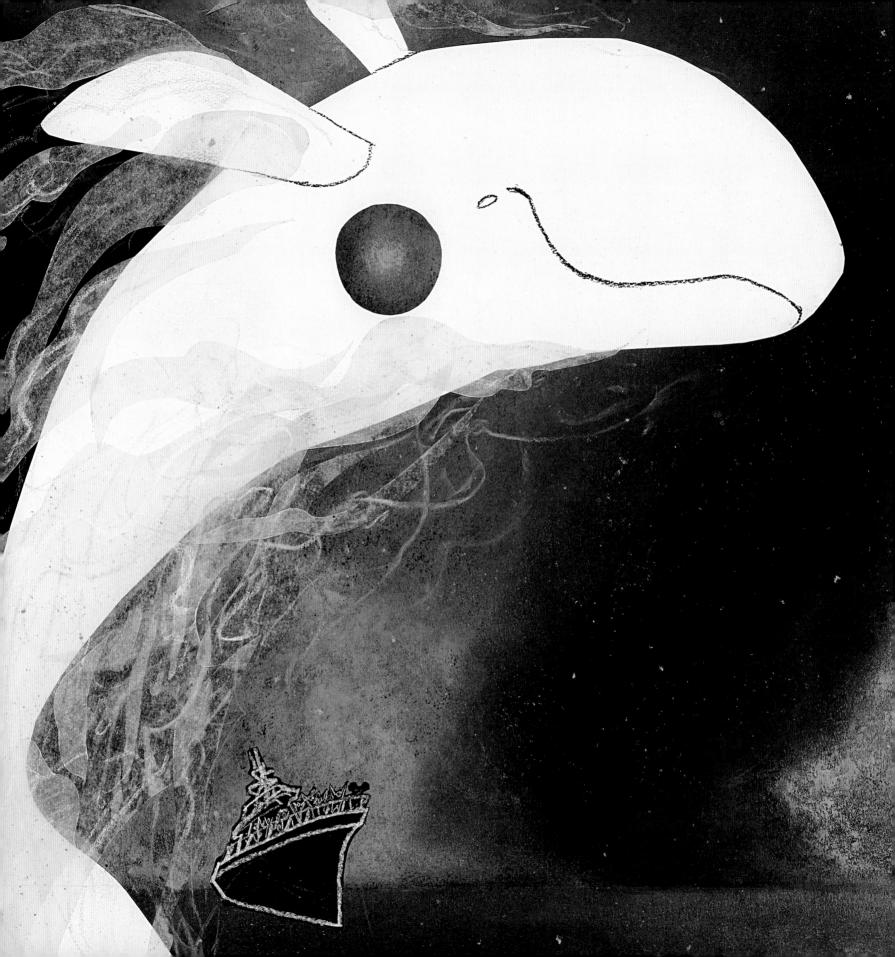

Two hearts,

one song.

One song. One light.

One hundred lights.

One thousand lights.

One million lights.

One world,
one song,
one heartbeat.

Author's Note

In 2014 I was one of several people selected to sail aboard the last wooden whaleship in the world, the *Charles W. Morgan*, after a painstaking, piece-by-piece restoration at Mystic Seaport. Along with my fellow illustrators in Dalvero Academy, I made art and documented the restoration through drawing from 2009 until the ship's return to the water in 2013. This, its thirty-eighth voyage, was a symbolic journey, traveling the whaling ports of the Northeast and transforming the ship from an agent of commercial brutality into one of environmental education and preservation. On our sail into Stellwagen Bank National Marine Sanctuary, whales were spotted from the deck of the *Morgan* for the first time in nearly 150 years, this time from a ship bringing a message of peace. It was this experience that lead to the creation of *Heartbeat*.

During the nineteenth century, commercial whaling was one of the largest American industries. Whales were killed and harvested in enormous numbers for their oil, their baleen (used for many of the things we use plastic for today), and their meat. It was a brutal and savage industry, for the men at sea as well as the whales. Often whale calves were orphaned and became completely lost, lingering around the whaleships.

Heartbeat follows the life of one whale calf whose mother is killed during this age of American whaling. For nearly two hundred years, we follow her through all the different ways that humans used whales to advance themselves: whale oil as an illuminant, as a lubricant during the industrial revolution and for machine guns in World War I, and in nitroglycerine explosives in World War II; and whale meat feeding millions of hungry people after the World Wars. In 1966, the Lunar Orbiter gave the world the first images of the surface of the moon and its view of the Earth. The images were recorded on tapes lubricated with whale oil. The whales became a prism through which humanity interacted with the universe.

But as history barreled on, our attitude toward whales began to shift. In 1977 NASA launched the *Voyager* spacecraft with a Golden Record, containing our own songs as well as the songs of humpback whales, as a message to any other life that might be out there. In 1983, the International Whaling Commission put a moratorium on commercial whaling to protect whales around the world. And since the 1990s, scientific research and whale-watching tourism have greatly increased our appreciation of the beauty, intelligence, and majesty of whales. Despite this progress, a few nations still engage in whaling, and the international disregard for the health of our oceans is even more damaging.

Whales live in a world of water and sound with very little distinction between themselves and the world, and so *Heartbeat* opens with very soft, fluid imagery without boundaries. But human vision is based on clear edges, so the human world is made out of cut paper. It's a visual distinction to show how different our worlds are. When the little girl hears the whale's song and joins in, she shows that pain can be a window into empathy if we choose. The collective song of compassion becomes solace for the baby whale and for the world. The song grows, and the edges between us start to dissolve. As more and more people join in the song, we all become united by that one thing we all share: a heartbeat.

For my teachers
Veronica Lawlor and Margaret Hurst,
who taught me
to see the world as an artist

ATHENEUM BOOKS FOR YOUNG READERS • An imprint of Simon & Schuster Children's Publishing Division • 1230 Avenue of the Americas, New York, New York 10020 • Copyright © 2018 by Evan Turk • All rights reserved, including the right of reproduction in whole or in part in any form. • ATHENEUM BOOKS FOR YOUNG READERS is a registered trademark of Simon & Schuster, Inc. • Atheneum logo is a trademark of Simon & Schuster, Inc. • For information about special discounts for bulk purchases, please contact Simon & Schuster Special Sales at 1-866-506-1949 or business@simonandschuster.com. • The Simon & Schuster Speakers Bureau can bring authors to your live event. For more information or to book an event, contact the Simon & Schuster Speakers Bureau at 1-866-248-3049 or visit our website at www.simonspeakers.com. • Book design by Ann Bobco • The text for this book was set in Requiem Text HTF Roman. • The illustrations for this book were rendered in pastel and charcoal on black paper, collage, and tracing paper. • Manufactured in China • 0318 SCP • First Edition • 10 9 8 7 6 5 4 3 2 1 • Library of Congress Cataloging-in-Publication Data • Names: Turk, Evan, author, illustrator. • Title: Heartbeat / Evan Turk. • Description: First edition. | New York : Atheneum, [2018] | Summary: Separated from her mother, a young whale swims the oceans for decades until she finds a young girl who shares her vision of one planet for which all are responsible. • Identifiers: LCCN 2017021527 (print) | LCCN 2017037361 (eBook) • ISBN 9781481435208 (hardcover) | ISBN 9781481435215 (eBook) • Subjects: | CYAC: Whales—Fiction. | Environmental protection—Fiction. • Classification: LCC PZ7.1.T874 (eBook) | LCC PZ7.1.T874 He 2018 (print) | DDC [E]—dc23 • LC record available at https://lccn.loc.gov/2017021527